FOR EMMA, ELSIE AND EMILE - M.R.
WITH THANKS TO CUMBERLAND SCHOOL - N.L.

Bloomsbury Publishing, London, New Delhi, New York and Sydney
First published in Great Britain in 2015 by Bloomsbury Publishing Plc
50 Bedford Square, London, WC1B 3DP

Text copyright © Michael Rosen 2015
Illustrations copyright © Neal Layton 2015
The moral rights of the author and illustrator have been asserted

A CIP catalogue record of this book is available from the British Library

ISBN 978 1 4088 4696 4 (PB)
ISBN 978 1 4088 4695 7 (eBook)

Printed in China by Leo Paper Products, Heshan, Guangdong

1 3 5 7 9 10 8 6 4 2

All papers used by Bloomsbury Publishing are natural, recyclable products
made from wood grown in well-managed forests.
The manufacturing processes conform to the environmental regulations of the country of origin

www.bloomsbury.com

BLOOMSBURY is a registered trademark of Bloomsbury Publishing Plc

Monster

Michael Rosen   Neal Layton

BLOOMSBURY

LONDON NEW DELHI NEW YORK SYDNEY

Hello. Just in case you don't know, I write books.
Today I want to tell you about something really, really scary.

I look after a small human. I call her Rover.
Here she is scratching the top of her head.

There are some other people I look after too.

Here's Rover's dad, Rex, who is quite nice
but he barks too much.

This is Rover's mum, Cindy.

She used to listen to me but nowadays seems
to be too busy with someone else.

That's someone who howls
and howls and howls.
That's why I call her Howler.

Next door, there are some small animals.

They know who I am.

Now for that really, really, REALLY scary thing.

One morning, Rex and Cindy started running round and round in circles.

They kept opening the drawer and then closing it.
I tried to help by telling them where my dinner is.

Then all of a sudden they rushed for the door.

Then they started sniffing around for something else.

I knew what they wanted: the stick – the one they keep losing.

But no, it wasn't what they wanted. Instead, they told me
to stay indoors, and they all rushed out with Rover.

I realised straight away that something was going on.
But what?

I waited and I waited and then out of the window
I saw Rex and Cindy and Howler coming back.

But no Rover!!! Rover wasn't with them.
They had left her somewhere!
How COULD they?

In a flash, I knew what to do.
The moment the door opened . . .

. . . I raced out to find Rover.

Maybe you don't know, but I have an amazingly super nose.
I can smell where people have been.

And it wasn't long before I found
where they had taken Rover . . .

. . . to a place where hundreds of
other small humans are kept.
I looked up at the cage and quickly saw a way in.

The small humans were very pleased to see me.
I couldn't see Rover so I thought she must be inside.
When the door opened, I rushed in.

I ran along the corridor, up the stairs, into the toilets
and out again, along another corridor.

And then I saw her.

She was stuck in the corner of a big room.
And she was surrounded by . . . horrible THINGS.
And there was one really big one. A HUGE monster.

I called out to Rover.
"I'm coming to save you from the Monster!"

I knew what I had to do. I flew through the air to save her.

But it went a bit wrong.

Rover did a lot of squeezing and patting.

Just then Rex and Cindy
turned up and grabbed me.

And then Howler started howling. Very loudly.
So I thought I'd better help keep her quiet.

I did that wagging-tail thing which Howler seems to like.
And everyone else seemed to like it too.

And I let Rex pat me.

He had the stick in his bag and I was worried he might
lose it again, so I followed them out of the door.

As Rover was having such a nice time,
I reckoned she'd be all right without me for a bit.
And I was right.
Not long after, she came back home to see me . . .

. . . just like she always does.